THE WHITE MARBLE

by

Charlotte Zolotow

Illustrated by Lilian Obligado

It was a hot night. John Henry was wide awake. Skipping between his parents he knew it was special to be allowed out in the park at night when the lamps shown down on the paths. A little girl from school, Pamela, was there, too, but she seemed different. They ran. They kicked their legs in the grass, saying nothing. John Henry had found a white marble and on this moment in the moonlight, they enjoyed its beauty. Before leaving the park, he gave her his treasured possession. They had shared a wonderful experience.

K

Classification and Dewey Decimal: Easy (E)

About the Author:

CHARLOTTE ZOLOTOW learned to read before she went to school and cannot remember the time when she did not want to write and illustrate books for children. She attended the University of Wisconsin where she met and married Maurice Zolotow, the writer. She was encouraged to write her first book by an editor with whom she worked and subsequently herself became an editor of juvenile books in a large publishing house. Many of her books grow out of stories she tells her own children.

About the Illustrator:

LILIAN OBLIGADO was born in Buenos Aires, Argentina, and attended art school there. For several years she lived on a ranch in the Argentine pampas where she had many animals as subjects. Miss Obligado now lives in New York City.

The White Marble

The White Marble

by Charlotte Zolotow

pictures by Lilian Obligado

1966 FIRST CADMUS EDITION
THIS SPECIAL EDITION
IS PUBLISHED BY ARRANGEMENT WITH
THE PUBLISHERS OF THE REGULAR EDITION
ABELARD-SCHUMAN LIMITED
BY

E. M. HALE AND COMPANY
EAU CLAIRE, WISCONSIN

© Copyright 1963 by Charlotte Zolotow / Library of Congress Catalogue
Card Number: 63-16215

This edition lithographed in U. S. A. by Wetzel Bros., Inc., Milwaukee 2, Wisconsin

Oh it was a hot night. The heat sat like a feathered bird over the city as the sun went down. It folded its wings and the pink and orange plumage of the sunset was covered by the fleecy grey and purple sky.

Not a breath stirred. John Henry's thin white bedroom curtain hung lifeless, dropped in absolutely still folds down along the side of his window. It had hung so in the sunlight all afternoon. Even John Henry had found it too hot then to do anything but sleep. Now that supper was finished, and the heat was still hovering over everything, his mother and father decided they would all go out to the park.

He was wide awake. His mother
looked tired. His father looked
tired. But the hot city night seemed
beautiful to John Henry as he
skipped along between them.

There wasn't a star in the
darkening sky.

A beautiful zigzag of lightning
cut across the park ahead of them.

"Perhaps it will rain," said John
Henry's father.

"I'm afraid that's the heat," his
mother said.

Their voices seemed far away
to John Henry.

They crossed the street and just as they
reached the dusky park, John Henry stopped.
He let go of his mother's hand and stooped
down to pick up something in the grass. He
stared at it for a minute with clear brown eyes
and then slipped it quickly into his pocket.

"What'd you find, John?" his father asked.

"Nothing," said John Henry walking now
a little ahead of his mother and father into
the park.

When they found a bench to themselves
John Henry sat between the grownups.

Two old men had a checkerboard open
between them on a bench that was directly
beneath the lamplight. The smoke from their
pipes coiled slowly upwards, cloudy and blue,
and the scent of tobacco mingled with the
nighttime smell of park grass. The branches
of the trees, close to the lamplight, seemed
to be rustling with golden leaves.

And John Henry was the only child in
the park.

He listened to the hot nighttime hum of grown-up voices. Even sitting here, between his mother and father, John Henry felt alone. But he knew it was special to be allowed out now and he sat like them, pretending to be grown up like them, but all the time his eyes searched and searched in the distance where the golden light of the lamps shone down on the park paths.

Then, far down the path, there came something white. He leaned forward – it was true – a white dress gleamed in the darkness and moved toward them slowly like a white moth until, at last, just across from their own bench, a mother and little girl sat down.

It was Pamela from school. He watched her spread
out her dress on either side like white wings, just
as she did at school when Miss Dawson had them
bring their chairs around for story time. But tonight
Pamela was different.

As he watched her, his hand stole up to his pocket again and he smiled.

She saw him and smiled too, and to him it was as though she had said, "I understand. They are grown up, but we *know,* we see what tonight is really like."

Suddenly he stood up.

"Let's run," he called, and without waiting
to see if she was following, he cut over
behind the benches, across the darkening park.
He could hear the soft echo of her footsteps
skimming over the grass behind him.

They kicked off their shoes and were off,
bare legs flashing. Like two small wild things,
intoxicated with the soft cool smell of rain
about to come, they ran together. Never, never
had the air smelled so fresh and sweet, never,
never had the night seemed so lovely before.

It belonged to them. Even when at last
they flung themselves down panting on the soft
grass, with the heavy purple sky folding into
night above them, and the unceasing grown-up
murmur of laughter and voices around them,
they were alone.

They lay there kicking their legs up and
down behind them, saying nothing.
Suddenly John Henry touched her hand.

"Look," he said, and pulled a small white marble out of his pocket.

She reached out to finger it but he closed his fingers around it quickly.

"It's beautiful!" she said.

No grownup would have known.

They lay there, again kicking their legs up and down behind them in silence while the little rain wind ruffled their hair.

"Are you thirsty?" she asked.

They picked up their shoes and
started off to the water fountain.
They passed a clump of lilac bushes,
immense in the gathering darkness.
Pamela put her hand on John
Henry's arm until they turned the
corner, to where the water fountain
sprinkled up white and foamy
in the night.

They bent their heads together and they could feel each other's hair against their cheeks as the water bubbled up cold and sweet straight into their faces, wetting their skin, running down their necks, so that with the iciness of it they began to laugh.

"John Henry...." called his father.
"Pamela...." called her mother.
But neither of them heard.

"JOHN HENRY...."

"PAMELA...."

The grown-up voices trailed off, swept up in the rustling of the little storm wind that started the whole park moving and sighing with the flutter of hot dusty lamplit leaves.

"JOHN HENRY," his father called, "ice sticks . . ."

Without wiping the water from their faces, they ran back to the bench where their parents were waiting.

Sure enough, there, with the tinkling of little bells and merry lights gleaming like a miniature carnival, was the ice cream man's cart transformed from the everyday yellow wagon they knew. They sat side by side, their legs swinging as they ate the icy pineapple sticks.

Across from them now, John
Henry's father stretched his arm
along the bench and his mother
rested her head against it while
they talked to Pamela's mother.

"Time to go...."
the grownups finally said.

Pamela slipped off the bench
and took her mother's hand.
They started down the lamplit
path. Streak! streak! streak! went the
lightning now.

Suddenly Pamela broke loose and ran back.

"John Henry," she called.

He turned.

Her eyes were green and gold as
she looked at him.

"Good night," she said.

A streak of starlight jetted across
the dark sky.

John Henry stared at her.
He put his hand in his pocket and
pulled out the white marble. For
a moment it lay there on his palm
like a small white moon gleaming
in the half darkness. Then he
pressed it into Pamela's hand.

"Keep it," he said.

From far away came the rumble of summer thunder and there was already the patter of raindrops in the dusty leaves of the city trees.